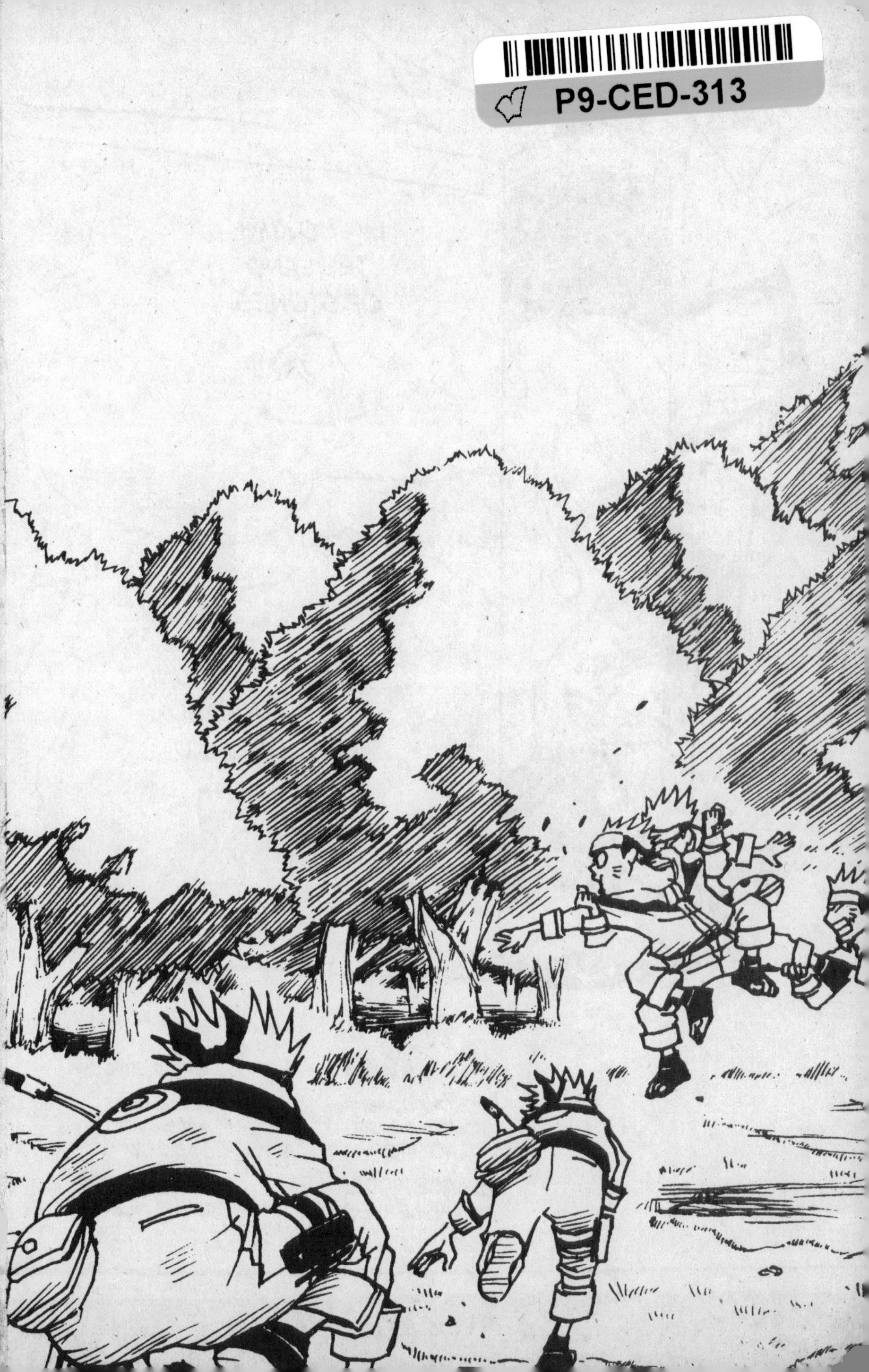

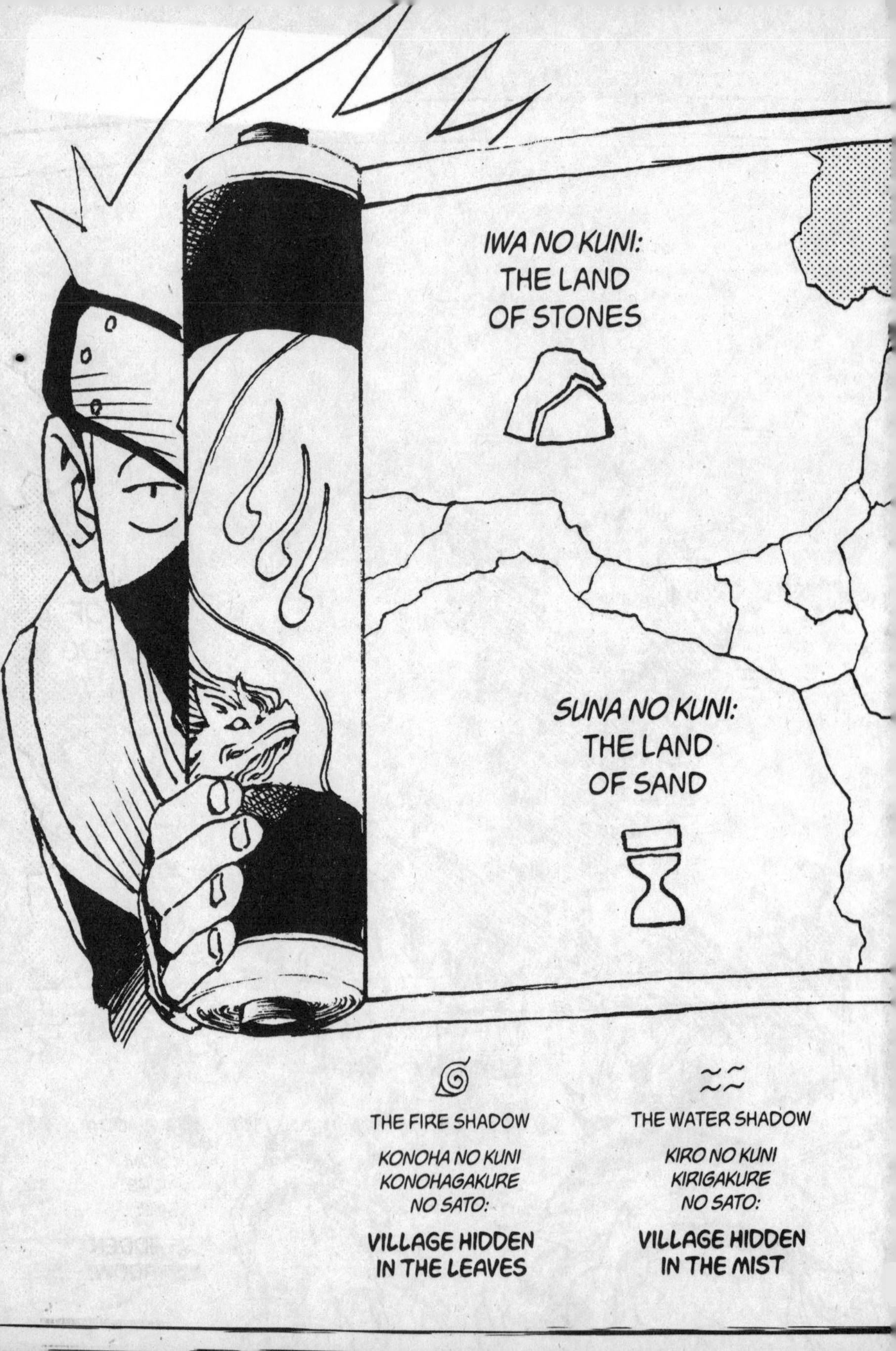

IWA NO KUNI:
THE LAND
OF STONES
SUNA NO KUNI:
THE LAND
OF SAND
THE FIRE SHADOW
KONOHA NO KUNI
KONOHAGAKURE
NO SATO:
VILLAGE HIDDEN
IN THE LEAVES
THE WATER SHADOW
KIRO NO KUNI
KIRIGAKURE
NO SATO:
VILLAGE HIDDEN
IN THE MIST

KUMO NO KUNI:
THE LAND OF
THE CLOUDS

KIRO NO KUNI:
THE LAND OF
MIST AND FOG

KONOHA NO KUNI:
THE LAND OF
TREE AND LEAF

THE LIGHTNING SHADOW

KUMO NO KUNI
KUMOGAKURE
NO SATO:

**VILLAGE HIDDEN
IN THE CLOUDS**

THE WIND SHADOW

SUNA NO KUNI
SUNAGAKURE
NO SATO:

**VILLAGE HIDDEN
IN THE SAND**

THE EARTH SHADOW

IWA NO KUNI
IWAGAKURE
NO SATO:

**VILLAGE HIDDEN
IN THE SHADOW**

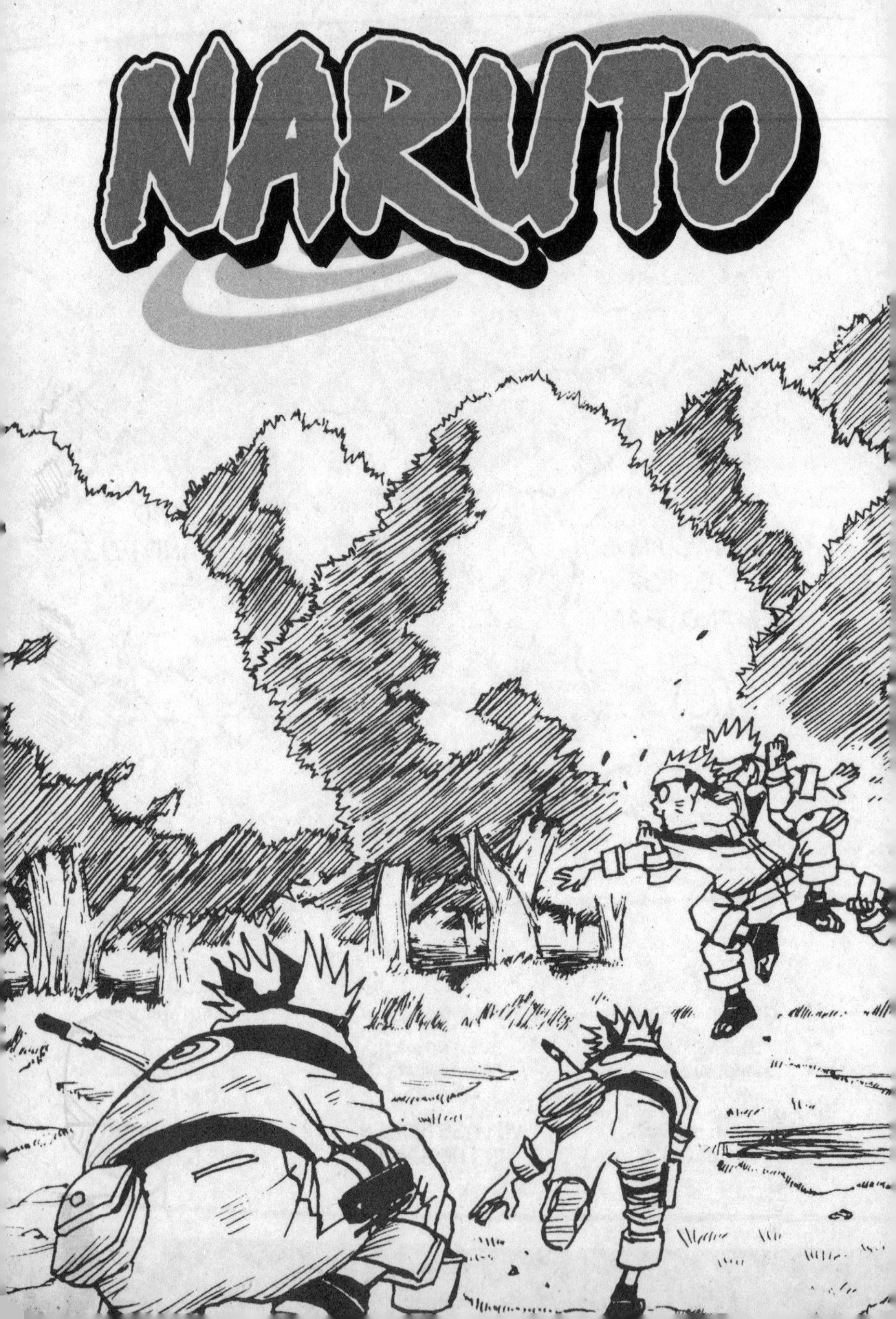
NARUTO

THE TESTS OF A NINJA

ORIGINAL STORY BY **MASASHI KISHIMOTO**

ADAPTED BY TRACEY WEST

vizkids

VIZ MEDIA

SAN FRANCISCO

NARUTO THE TESTS OF A NINJA
CHAPTER BOOK 2

Illustrations: Masashi Kishimoto
Design: Courtney Utt

NARUTO © 1999 by Masashi Kishimoto. All rights reserved.
Original manga first published in Japan in 1999 by SHUEISHA Inc., Tokyo. This
English language chapter book novelization is based on the original manga.

Published by VIZ Media, LLC
P.O. Box 77010
San Francisco, CA 94107

www.viz.com

West, Tracey, 1965-
 The tests of a ninja / original story by Masashi Kishimoto ; adapted by Tracey West.
 p. cm.
 Summary: Instead of receiving an exciting mission after graduating from the Ninja Academy, prankster
Naruto must train with the old master Kakashi, from whom he learns the importance of teamwork.
 ISBN 978-1-4215-2213-5
 [1. Ninja—Fiction. 2. Teamwork (Sports)—Fiction. 3. Japan—Fiction.]
 I. Kishimoto, Masashi. II. Title. PZ7.W51937Tf 2008
 [Fic]—dc22
     2008006169

Printed in the U.S.A.
First printing, October 2008
Third printing, March 2022

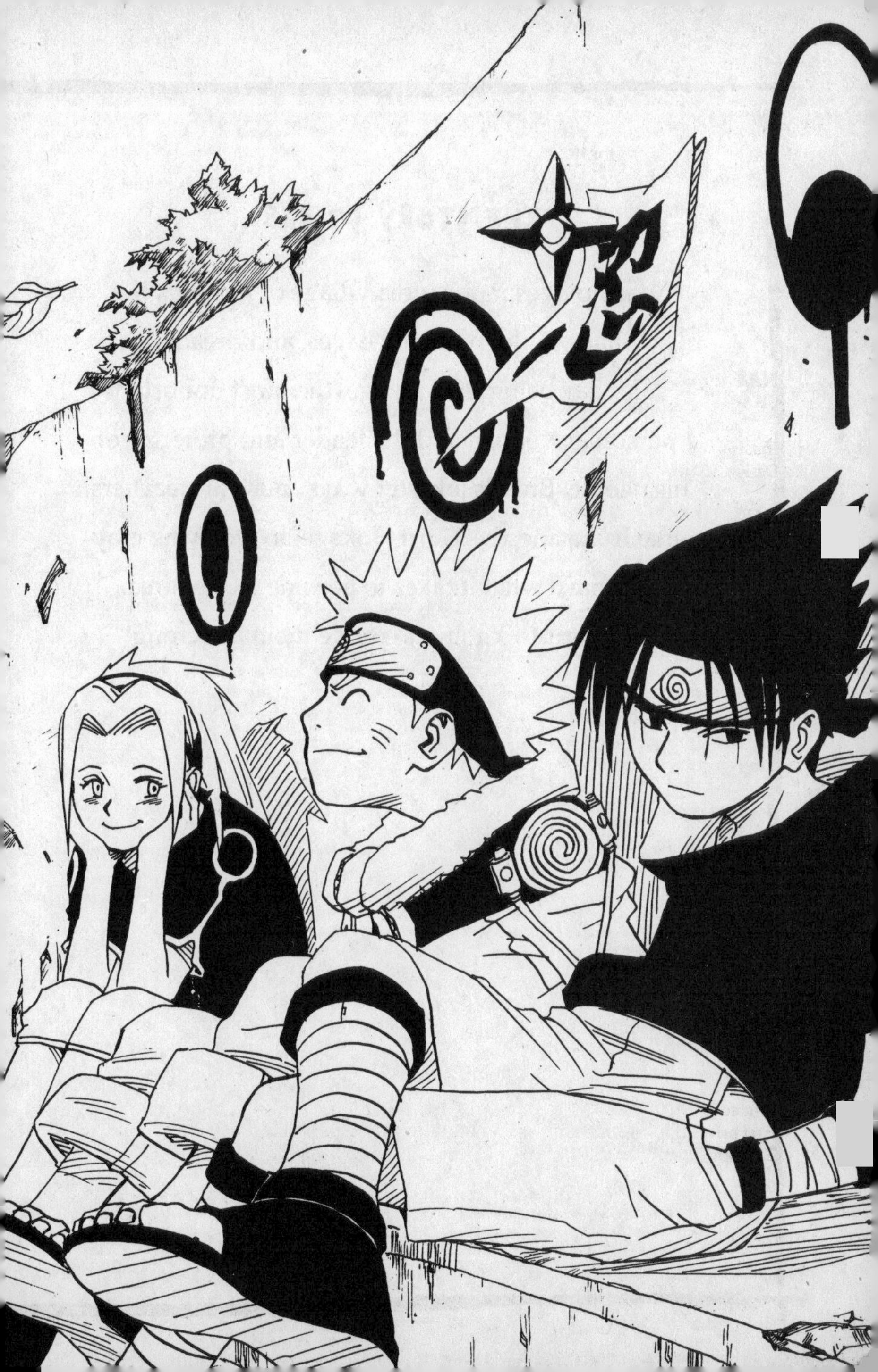

THE STORY SO FAR...

Naruto lives in the ninja village of Konoha, the Village Hidden in the Leaves, and dreams of someday being the Hokage, the most important person in Konoha and the leader and protector of his people. But his jokester ways cause his teachers, like Iruka and the Third Hokage, to worry he may not have what it takes to become a true ninja. But Naruto's going to prove them all wrong!

Naruto
ナルト

Naruto is training to be a ninja. He's a bit of a clown. But deep down, he's serious about becoming the world's greatest shinobi!

The Third Hokage
三代目火影

The most respected person in the village is known as the Hokage.

Iruka
イルカ

Naruto's former teacher at the Academy. He's the one who finally told Naruto that when Naruto was a baby, the spirit of a fox demon was sealed deep inside of him.

1

NARUTO UZUMAKI woke up, drank a glass of milk, and shuffled into his bathroom. He looked into the mirror and yawned. His reflection stared back at him. The blond, spiky hair that he never brushed. The marks on his cheeks he'd had since he was born that looked almost like whiskers. And the dark circles under his blue eyes, because he had stayed up late—again.

He quickly got dressed and tied his leaf headband around his head. The headband meant that Naruto was a real ninja.

Now his serious ninja training would begin.

He ran all the way to the academy. When he got to his class, he slid into his seat behind his desk. One of his classmates marched up to him.

"What are you doing here, Naruto? I thought you failed the graduation test."

Naruto leaned back in his seat. "I got my leaf headband, didn't I?" he said smugly. He *had* failed the test. But then Naruto had saved his teacher from a ninja master named

Mizuki. Naruto had earned his leaf headband that day.

"Excuse me, may I pass?"

Naruto looked past the boy to see a girl with pale pink hair standing there. He blushed. "Hi, Sakura."

She wants to sit next to me! No way, Naruto thought. Sakura was the prettiest girl in Ninja Academy.

But Sakura pushed past him. "Naruto, move it! I'm trying to get around you!"

Sakura sat down at her desk and gazed dreamily at Sasuke Uchiha, who was sitting two seats away from Naruto. She wasn't interested in Naruto at all. Naruto glared at dark-haired Sasuke. There wasn't a stain or wrinkle in his blue shirt and white pants.

Everybody thought Sasuke was so perfect—especially the girls in class. Just because he aced every test. So what?

Master Iruka came into the classroom. The teacher, or sensei, had taught the students for many years. Naruto sat up straight. Finally, things were going to get started.

But Master Iruka had a big lecture to give, like always.

"From this day on, you are all ninja," Iruka began. "But right now you are genin, the lowest of the low. Your greatest challenges still lie ahead."

Naruto slumped down in his seat, bored.

Master Iruka continued. "You will soon be given official duties to help out the village," he said. "But first, you will be split up into three-man squads. A jonin, a higher ranking ninja, will lead each squad. Your jonin will coach you as you perform your duties."

Naruto perked up a bit. Three-man squads could be interesting.

If I get to be in a squad with Sakura it won't matter who the third person is, he thought. *I'll take anybody else—except Sasuke.*

Next to him, Sakura was lost in a daydream. *I've **got** to be on Sasuke's squad! I've **got** to!*

At the end of the row, Sasuke frowned. *Three-man squads? Sounds like two too many…*

Iruka picked up a clipboard. "I've made up the squads so the skills in each one are even," he said. "First, Squad One."

The teacher read off the first six squads.

Naruto did not hear his name. Then Iruka read out the names for Squad Seven.

"Sakura Haruno," he began. Naruto crossed his fingers for luck. "Naruto Uzumaki."

"Woo-hoo!" Naruto cried out.

Sakura scowled. **_Rats!_**

Then Iruka called out the final name. "Sasuke Uchiha."

Sakura jumped up. **_OH YEAH!_**

"Master Iruka, what were you thinking? How could you stick an excellent ninja like me with that loser?" Naruto pointed at Sasuke. Sakura scowled at him.

"There are twenty-seven people in this class," Iruka said. His voice was stern. "Sasuke has the best grades. You, Naruto, have the worst. The idea is to have a balance of strengths in each squad. That is why I put you together."

Sasuke glanced at Naruto. "Just don't drag me down," he said. "You're a dunce."

Naruto clenched his fists. "What did you call me?"

Before either of them could say another word, their teacher announced, "Your jonin will be here soon." Inside, Iruka thought, *Awww, they'll work it out. Even Naruto...*

2

THE CLASS WAITED for their jonin to arrive. One by one, each squad left with its new sensei. Only Squad Seven was left. Bored, Naruto put an eraser on top of the door. When the jonin opened the door, the eraser would fall on his head—a classic prank.

And that's exactly what happened. A few minutes later, a tall ninja opened the door.

BAM! The eraser fell on his head.

"Ha!" Naruto laughed. He pointed at the ninja, who was covered with chalk dust. "Gotcha! Good one!"

The ninja didn't move. He stared at the students with one dark eye. His leaf headband was slanted down and covered the other eye. A black cloth hid the lower half of his face. He wore a green vest over a black shirt and pants. His white hair stuck out of his headband like long blades of grass.

"I'm sorry, Sensei," Sakura said nervously. She thought the trick had been totally awesome—but didn't want to get in trouble. "I tried to stop him, but Naruto wouldn't listen."

Sasuke didn't say anything—out loud. *So this is our skilled ninja leader?* he thought. *How could he fall for such a stupid trick?*

"Let me see," the teacher said. He tapped a finger on his chin, thinking. "How shall I put this? Based on my first impression, I have to say...I really don't like students like you!"

Naruto's smile faded. Was he going to get in trouble—again?

But the jonin turned toward the door. "Follow me," he said simply.

They followed their new squad leader to an outdoor garden on the roof of the Ninja Academy. Rows of shady trees grew under rows of large metal arches. Naruto, Sasuke and Sakura sat on the steps in front of the trees. Their teacher faced them. He leaned on a railing near the edge of the roof and folded his arms across his chest.

"I'd like you each to tell us about yourself," he said.

"Like what?" Sakura asked.

"You know, the usual," the teacher replied. "The thing you like the best. The thing you hate the most. Your dreams. Your hobbies. Things like that."

"Can you help us out here, coach?" Naruto asked. "Show us how it's done."

"That's right," Sakura added. "After all, you're a complete stranger to us."

"Okay," the teacher agreed. "My name is Kakashi Hatake. I don't like talking about what I like and dislike. My dreams for the future are none of your business. And...I have lots of hobbies."

Sakura sighed. "Well, he talked a lot, but all we really learned is his name."

"All right, now it's your turn," Kakashi said. He nodded at Naruto.

Naruto perked up.

"Me? I'm Naruto Uzumaki," he began. "What I like is instant ramen noodles in a cup. What I like even better is when Master Iruka treats me to ramen at the noodle restaurant. What I hate is the three-minute wait after I pour the boiling water on the noodles..."

Kakashi raised an eyebrow. *Does this kid think of anything besides ramen noodles?*

"Now let me tell you my dream," Naruto said. "My dream is to one day be a better ninja than **LORD HOKAGE!** Then all the villagers will have to show me respect."

Now, that's interesting, Kakashi thought. The Hokage was the village champion, the leader and the most respected person in the village. The Hokage was also usually the most powerful ninja.

"My hobbies are pranks and practical jokes, I guess," Naruto finished.

Kakashi scratched his head. What kind of student loved pranks yet dreamed of being the greatest ninja ever? "I see," he said. "Next!"

Sasuke stared straight ahead as he spoke. "My name is Sasuke Uchiha," he began. "There are plenty of things I hate. There is almost nothing that I like. It seems stupid to talk about dreams, because that's just a word."

Sasuke's voice was low and serious. "What I do have is a goal. I plan to restore my clan. And there is someone I have sworn to **DESTROY.**"

I hope it's not me, Naruto thought.

But Kakashi just nodded.

"And finally, the young lady," Kakashi said, nodding at Sakura.

Sakura was looking over at Sasuke, blushing.

"I am Sakura Haruno," she said. "The

thing I like best isn't really a thing...it's a person. I mean, it's a boy." Her cheeks turned bright red.

"Um, let's move on to my dream," she continued. She glanced at Sasuke. Then she blushed again. "I can't talk about that. So let's see...What I hate is...Naruto!"

"What?!" Naruto cried out.

Sakura didn't seem to care that she had hurt his feelings. "Okay, my hobbies are..."

"Enough!" Kakashi said. "I think we all understand each other. Your formal training starts tomorrow."

Naruto jumped up. "Yes, sir!" he said, giving a salute. "Our first real ninja mission! What do we have to do?"

"Our first project involves only the

members of this squad," Kakashi answered.

"WHAT? What is it?" Naruto asked impatiently. Even Sasuke looked excited.

OUR FIRST PROJECT INVOLVES ONLY THE MEMBERS OF THIS CELL.

Kakashi lowered his head. "It's a survival exercise." He started to laugh.

"What's so funny?" Sakura demanded.

"Oh nothing," Kakashi replied. "It's just that, if I told you, you would chicken out."

Naruto was starting to get annoyed with his new sensei. Why wouldn't he just get to the point? "WHY would we chicken out?"

"There are twenty-seven members of your graduating class," Kakashi explained. "Only nine of you will be accepted as junior-level ninja. The other eighteen must go back to Ninja Academy for more training. Most of the students who take this test **do not pass.**"

Another test? Back to the academy? It wasn't fair! Naruto wanted to scream. Sakura and Sasuke didn't look happy either.

Kakashi saw their faces and laughed. "See? You're chickening out already!"

Naruto exploded. "That stinks! We already took our final graduation test!" he yelled. "Doesn't that count?"

Kakashi shrugged. "We want to weed out the worst students. The ones who are left will make the best ninja," he went on. "We will meet tomorrow morning on the practice field. Bring all of your ninja tools and weapons. And don't eat breakfast...unless you like throwing up."

Sakura turned pale. "How hard is this test going to be?"

But Naruto wasn't worried. *I am going to pass that test tomorrow. No way will I go back to Ninja Academy!* he told himself. *I'll show Master Kakashi. Then everyone will respect me!*

3

NARUTO, SAKURA, AND SASUKE walked onto
the practice field early the next morning. Tall
trees surrounded the grassy field. The sun
was slowly rising into the blue sky.

Naruto's stomach growled. "I'm hungry
already," he complained. "I hope this stupid
test won't take too long."

Sakura looked around the field. "Where is
Master Kakashi, anyway?"

"Good morning, class!"

The three students looked up. Kakashi
had appeared in the middle of the field, like

magic. He wasn't there a second ago.

"YOU'RE LATE!" Naruto and Sakura yelled.

Kakashi stood next to an old tree stump. He put an alarm clock on the stump.

"This alarm will go off at noon," he said calmly. Then he held up two tiny bells. Each bell hung from a short string. "Your challenge is to steal these bells from me before the alarm sounds."

Kakashi attached the bells to his belt. "If you fail, you won't get any lunch," he went on. "Instead, you will be tied to that tree stump while I eat your lunch in front of you."

"So that's why you told us to skip breakfast!" Naruto wailed.

"You just need to take one bell from me to get your lunch," Kakashi said. "But as you can see, there are only two bells, and three of you. One of you is going to fail this test. Whoever fails will be going back to school."

Kakashi's words made Naruto extra determined to pass the test. Sakura's eyes grew wide. She looked nervous. Sasuke's whole body looked tense, as if he were ready to spring into action.

"You may use weapons if you want," Kakashi continued. "Attack me as though you want to destroy me. That's the only way you'll win."

"But that's so dangerous!" Sakura cried. Each ninja knew how to use shuriken, ninja throwing stars. They also carried kunai—small, sharp knives. Sakura had always imagined using them against an enemy. How could she hurl a throwing star against her own teacher?

Naruto just laughed. "You couldn't even dodge an eraser!" he taunted. "You're gonna get yourself killed!"

"Must you talk so big?" Kakashi replied calmly. "Only the weak speak loudly. Now let's forget this dunce. We will start on my signal."

Anger rose up inside Naruto. Dunce? How dare the sensei call him a dunce? His right hand quickly moved to the kunai strapped in a holster on his thigh. He pulled one out. With a loud cry, he charged at Kakashi.

He was just a few steps away from the teacher when he felt a hand on top of his head. Smack! Then another hand quickly pulled back his right arm. Kakashi held Naruto firmly. He couldn't move. And even worse—his own kunai was now pointed at the back of his head!

"Not so fast," Kakashi said, his voice cool. "I didn't say 'go' yet."

WOW, Sakura thought. *I didn't even see Sensei move.*

Even Sasuke was impressed. *So he is a*

skilled ninja after all. A real jonin.

"At least you struck to destroy," Kakashi told Naruto. "That means you're starting to respect me. And maybe…just maybe…I'm starting to like you three."

The sensei let go of Naruto. "Now it's time to start," he said. "Ready…set…*GO!*"

4

The members of Squad Seven ran in all directions. Within seconds, they had vanished among the trees.

"Every ninja learns how to become invisible," Kakashi said to himself. "Let's see how well these three have learned."

He scanned the field. He couldn't hear a sound except the birds in the trees. He didn't see any leaves moving. He nodded. "They are well hidden."

Then a loud cry broke the silence.

"It's time to bring it on!" Naruto shouted.

He jumped into the field. "Let's go!"

"I think you're making the wrong move, Naruto," Kakashi said calmly.

"Yeah? Well the only thing wrong here is your haircut!" Naruto shot back. Then he ran at Kakashi.

Kakashi slowly reached into a small pouch attached to his belt. Naruto skidded to a stop.

"Uh-oh!" he cried. Was Kakashi going for a weapon?

"Let me teach you the First Shinobi Battle Skill," Kakashi said. "*Taijutsu*: the art of the trained body."

Art of the trained body—isn't that hand-to-hand fighting? Naruto wondered. *So why is he reaching for a weapon?*

Kakashi's hand came out of the pouch. He wasn't holding a weapon. It was a book!

Naruto squinted. The book's title was *Make-Out Paradise*. Naruto stopped in his tracks. He was confused.

"Is something wrong?" Kakashi asked. "I thought you were coming for me."

"Yeah, but…I mean…what's up with that book?" Naruto asked.

"Well, I want to find out how the story ends," Kakashi said. "Go ahead and attack. I can fight you and read this at the same time."

Naruto couldn't believe it. This was the ultimate insult!

"I'm gonna flatten you!" Naruto yelled. He charged ahead and aimed his best punch at Kakashi's face. Kakashi batted Naruto's fist away with his free hand.

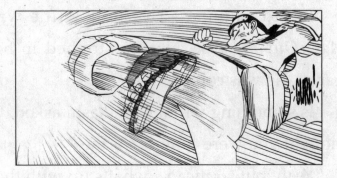

Naruto didn't give up. He jumped high in the air, his left leg extended in a powerful kick. Kakashi quickly crouched down, avoiding the blow. He never took his eyes off the book.

That only made Naruto more furious. "All right, that's it!" he cried. He hurled his body at Kakashi with all his strength.

He stopped. Kakashi was gone. But where was he?

Then Naruto heard the jonin's voice behind him. "You really should stop turning your back to your enemy," Kakashi said. "That's bad ninjutsu, dunce."

Sakura and Sasuke watched the battle from their hiding places. Sakura saw Kakashi making a strange sign with his hands. His palms were pressed together, and his first and middle fingers were pointed forward.

He's making the sign of the tiger, Sakura realized. *That's super advanced ninjutsu. He can't use that on Naruto!*

Then their teacher made the sign of flames. Sasuke saw it too. Kakashi wasn't fooling around. Sasuke sighed.

Sakura forgot she was supposed to be hiding. She called out to Naruto.

"Naruto, get out of there!"

Naruto turned at the sound of her voice.

"What?"

"Too late," Kakashi said calmly. "You are about to experience the most secret technique in Leaf Village. One Thousand Years of Death!"

Naruto tried to run, but before he could get away, Kakashi reached out and poked him hard.

"*Aaaaaaaah!*" The powerful poke sent Naruto flying across the field. He landed with a splash in the middle of a pond.

Kakashi turned back to his book and kept reading. Down in the pond, Naruto struggled to swim to the top.

This is not *how it's gonna go*, Naruto told

himself. He reached for two throwing stars in his pockets. With all his strength, he hurled them out of the water.

The shuriken swiftly flew toward Kakashi. Without looking, the jonin reached out. He caught one shuriken on one finger. The other shuriken landed on another finger. Kakashi kept reading the whole time.

Naruto kept swimming. *I WILL NOT BACK DOWN!* he thought. His ninja gear was weighing him down, but he didn't give up. He jumped out of the water and landed on the field.

Then he fell to his knees, coughing. He had swallowed a lot of water in that pond. His muscles ached.

"Well, what are you waiting for?" Kakashi

asked. "You just need to get one of these bells by noon, so you can have lunch."

"*Duh,*" Naruto said. "I know that!"

"You want to be a better ninja than Lord Hokage, but you've already run out of steam," Kakashi pointed out.

"I can fight you no matter how hungry I am," Naruto said angrily. "I just wasn't ready, that's all! You didn't give us time to prepare."

"A ninja is always prepared," Kakashi reminded him.

Naruto scowled. He knew the teacher was right. And that he had to get that bell—to earn Kakashi's respect.

"NO MATTER WHAT, I HAVE TO BECOME A TRUE NINJA!" Naruto cried.

He stood up, gathering all his energy. He raised his arms. Behind him, eight copies of Naruto rose up from the pond.

"Get a load of my specialty, the *ART OF THE DOPPELGANGER!*" Naruto cried. "Now you face a lot more than just one of me!"

The eight Narutos landed on the field behind him.

Sasuke couldn't believe what he was seeing. *Eight Narutos? What technique is he using?*

Sakura was amazed too. In the academy, they had all learned how to make doppelgangers—copies of themselves. But the copies were always illusions. Naruto's copies looked solid.

Kakashi's eyes widened in surprise.

Before he could react, a Naruto doppelganger jumped on his back from behind. The copy held Kakashi in a tight grip. Two of the other doppelgangers ran at Kakashi, gripping his legs.

"I had one of my copies climb out of the river, then sneak up on you," the real Naruto bragged. "But don't worry. I'll go easy on you."

He raised his fist to deliver a punch.

SMACK! He hit Kakashi in the face. Or did he? He looked down at his fist. Kakashi wasn't there. He was punching one of his own copies!

"What?" Naruto and the copy crashed to the ground.

"Ouch!" Naruto cried. He pushed the copy

off of him and jumped to his feet.

"You're Master Kakashi, aren't you?" he shouted, pointing. "You used a jutsu to change into me!"

"No, I didn't!" the copy shouted back.

"Yes, you did!" another copy yelled.

"No, you did!" another Naruto cried.

All nine Narutos began to fight, pushing and punching each other.

"Hey, wait a minute!" one of the Narutos said. "Just undo the jutsu. Then there will only be two of us. One will be the real you, and one will be Kakashi."

"Why didn't you think of that sooner?" Naruto snapped.

"Because I'm you, idiot!" the copy replied. "Just undo the jutsu already.'

"FINE!" Naruto shouted.

BONG! A loud sound rang through the trees. The nine Naruto copies disappeared. Only Naruto stood in the field.

Now Naruto was more confused than ever. He thought Kakashi had made himself look like Naruto. Naruto had gotten rid of his copies. So where was Kakashi? Could the jonin really move that fast?

From his hiding place, Sasuke watched the battle closely. He was beginning to understand Kakashi's strategy.

Kakashi used a replacement jutsu on Naruto, Sasuke realized. *It's an old ninja skill. You swap places with one of the plants, animals, or people around you. Your enemy thinks he's hitting you, but instead strikes the log or rock or whatever you've switched places with.*

In this case, Kakashi let one of the Naruto copies grab him. Then he swapped places with the copy. Naruto thought he was attacking Kakashi, but instead he attacked himself. Pretty good move.

Naruto brushed the dirt off of his pants. He was sore from the fight. But he still wasn't giving up. He had to get that bell.

And then, suddenly, there it was. A single silver bell shone in the grass under a tree.

"A bell!" Naruto cried. "I must have shaken up Kakashi pretty badly. He dropped it and didn't even notice!"

Naruto reached for the bell.

Suddenly, he felt something tug at his ankles.

"Hey!" he yelled. "What the…" His whole body was yanked into the air. Naruto was hung upside down from the tree branch. It was a trap!

5

KAKASHI STEPPED OUT in front of the tree. He reached down and picked up the bell.

"You used your technique well, but so did I," the sensei said. "Getting caught in such an obvious trap was stupid!"

Naruto growled. He did feel stupid.

"Ninja read the hidden meanings within hidden meanings," Kakashi told him.

"I know that already!" Naruto yelled.

"Uh, no, you don't," Kakashi pointed out. "That's why you're hanging upside down from a tree."

Sasuke watched the sensei and Naruto. Kakashi seemed to be completely off guard. Now was the time to make a move.

Sasuke swiftly jumped up on a tree branch and sent a storm of throwing stars flying through the air.

WHAP! WHAP! WHAP! Naruto was shocked to see the stars hitting Kakashi.

"Whoa! That was overkill, Sasuke!" Naruto cried out.

But all was not as it seemed. In fact, the shuriken had not hit Kakashi at all! The illusion of the ninja vanished. In its place was a log.

Sasuke was angry with himself. *Kakashi used a replacement jutsu again!* Sasuke fumed. *He just pretended to be off guard, and I fell for it!*

Now he knows my hiding place!

Sasuke dashed through the trees. His only hope was to run and hide before Kakashi heard him.

Sakura heard Sasuke move from his hiding place. Had Kakashi caught him? She didn't think about what might happen to her. She ran from her spot. She had to save Sasuke!

She saw a figure through the bushes and stopped, silent. Kakashi stood there, reading his book. He hadn't caught Sasuke. Sakura sighed with relief.

"Sakura, behind you!" a voice whispered.

She turned. Kakashi was standing right behind her!

"*Aaaaaaaaah!*" Sakura screamed. She'd been caught!

Back at the tree, Naruto reached for one of his kunai. He strained as he stretched up to cut the rope.

"Ha! Kakashi wants me to read the hidden meanings within hidden meanings," he muttered. "Well, I'm not gonna get caught in another one of his traps!"

Naruto jumped to the ground. He took a step forward—and landed right in another trap!

"Not again!" Naruto yelled as a rope tightened around his ankle. His body was yanked back into the air again.

Nearby, Sasuke thought he heard Sakura scream.

"Probably another one of Kakashi's tricks," Sasuke guessed out loud. "And she fell for it. Figures."

"The Second Shinobi Battle Skill, *genjutsu*: the art of illusion." Kakashi stepped out from behind a tree.

Sasuke smirked.

"I'm going to be on my guard from now on. I won't fall so easily. I'm not like Sakura and Naruto," Sasuke said.

"Say that after you get one of these bells, Sasuke." Kakashi chuckled. He took out his book again and began to read.

Sasuke turned and glared at the jonin.

"Prepare to face the strength of my clan," Sasuke said, his voice steady.

"The strength of the Uchiha Clan, the most elite family in the Leaf Village. I'm looking forward to it," Kakashi replied.

The two ninja studied each other. Then Sasuke made the first move. He quickly sent several shuriken flying through the air.

"It's no use attacking me from the front," Kakashi told him. Then he realized that the throwing stars weren't aimed at *him*. They were speeding toward a rope hanging from the trees.

"A trap?" Kakashi guessed. But he had figured it out in time. He jumped out of the way just as the rope released a dozen

throwing knives. The knives stuck into a tree trunk instead of him.

Not bad, Kakashi thought. And Sasuke had another surprise for him. The young ninja jumped over Kakashi and attacked him from behind. Kakashi stopped one powerful kick with his hand. But Sasuke kept coming. He aimed a punch at Kakashi's head.

Kakashi grabbed Sasuke's wrist and flipped him upside down. Sasuke reached out with his other arm, trying to take a bell. His fingertips touched one of the bells. But Kakashi quickly threw him off.

I guess I won't be able to finish Make-Out Paradise *now*, Kakashi thought. *Too bad!*

"I admit it," he told Sasuke. "You are not like the others."

Sasuke gathered all his energy together. He needed a move—a big one. He pressed his two index fingers together.

"Horse!" he said, naming the move.

Then he folded down his other fingers. "Tiger!" he shouted. ***"FIRE STYLE! FIREBALL TECHNIQUE!"***

Kakashi was shocked. *He's too young to do that move! It's not possible!*

FWOOOOOM!

Blazing waves of fire shot from Sasuke's hands. They raced across the field.

Then the fire went out. Sasuke waited for the smoke to clear. He expected to see Kakashi's body covered with ashes from the fire. But the jonin had vanished.

Where did he go? Sasuke spun around. *He's*

not behind me.

He looked up. *He's not above.*

A hand broke through the dirt, grabbing Sasuke's ankle.

"Earth Style!" Kakashi cried, as he pulled Sasuke down into the ground. "Groundhog Technique!"

Sasuke didn't get a chance to fight back. Soon he was buried up to his neck in dirt. Kakashi kneeled down in front of him.

"That was the Third Shinobi Battle Skill, *ninjutsu*. At least you performed better than those other two. But you know what they say, the nail that sticks up the most is the one that gets hammered down!"

Kakashi walked away, laughing. Sasuke scowled.

Back at the tree, Naruto was still hanging upside down. He had a good view of the tree stump and the alarm clock. Behind the stump, something caught his eye.

Hey, there are two lunch boxes on top of that boulder, he thought. *Perfect!* He quickly cut himself down. Then he ran to the lunch boxes, grabbed them both and sat down on the ground.

"I might not be able to get a bell fair and square," he said, opening the first box. "But at least I can still eat lunch!"

Suddenly, Kakashi jumped up on the boulder behind him. "Oh really?" he asked. He loomed over Naruto.

"Argh!" Naruto was caught red-handed.

"Uh, I was just kidding," Naruto stammered. But he knew it was no use. He was in big trouble now!

Not far away, Sakura woke up. After Master Kakashi caught her, strange things had happened. She thought she saw Sasuke's body on the ground, bruised and hurt. Then she had fainted. But where was Master Kakashi now? And what about Sasuke? She jumped to her feet.

"Sasuke is hurt!" she cried. "I've got to find him!"

She ran through the trees. Then she stopped. There was Sasuke's head, sticking out of the ground.

"Aaaaah!" she screamed. What happened to the rest of him?

Sasuke pulled himself out of the ground.

"You're okay!" Sakura threw her arms around Sasuke.

"Yeah, right," Sasuke said. "Time's running out. It's almost noon. I've got to go."

"Do you really think you can take one of those bells?" Sakura asked.

"I got close enough to touch them," Sasuke told her. "This time, I'll take them."

"Wow, that's amazing!" Sakura said. But she was secretly worried. If Sasuke got a bell, he would move on to his genin training. She would have to go back to school without him. That would be terrible!

"I really don't think there's enough time," Sakura pointed out. "Maybe we should just go back to the academy and try again next time."

Sasuke shrugged. "Give up if you want. I have an enemy I have sworn to destroy. But I can't do that if I'm stuck at the academy. So I'm not giving up."

He walked back to the practice field. Sakura followed him. They saw the tree stump up ahead. Naruto was tied to it, struggling to get free.

Then the clock struck twelve.

RIIIIIIIIING! went the alarm.

The test was over—and none of them had a bell!

6

"**OH LISTEN TO** your little stomachs growl," Kakashi said. "Looks like none of you earned your lunch. But I have more news for you."

Naruto looked up, trying to stay hopeful. Maybe they would get another chance?

"None of you will be going back to Ninja Academy," Kakashi said.

"Yeah!" Naruto cried. "That means we passed!"

"Even me, after I got fooled by that trick?" Sakura asked.

Sasuke was the only one who wasn't smiling. He knew this had to be another one of Kakashi's tricks. And he was right.

"You three are hopeless," Kakashi said. "None of you are going to be ninja, ever! **You might as well all give up now."**

"GIVE UP!" Naruto shouted. "What do you mean? So none of us got one of your stupid bells. Why should we quit over that?"

"Because none of you has what it takes," Kakashi said. He sounded serious. "You three mock the code of the ninja with your behavior. Don't you know why you were put into teams?"

"Uh, no…" Sakura answered.

"That's obvious," Kakashi said. "You missed the whole point of the test."

"There was a point?" Naruto asked.

"But that's not fair," Sakura said. "You didn't tell us what the point was."

"Yeah, tell us already!" Naruto shouted.

Kakashi sighed. "The test was about **teamwork!**" he shouted. "If the three of you had worked together, you might have been able to take the bells."

"But wait a minute," Sakura protested. "There are three of us, but two bells. Even if we had worked together, somebody would have been left out. You set this up so we'd fight with each other no matter what!"

"Exactly," Kakashi said. "That's why it's a test. A true team would have worked together, no matter what the cost. But you three only thought of yourselves."

Kakashi nodded at Sakura. "You could have helped Naruto when I trapped him, but you ran after Sasuke instead. Naruto tried to

do everything himself. And Sasuke decided he was better off without you two."

The jonin shook his head. The answer had been right in front of them all along, but they'd been too blind to see it.

"It's important for a ninja to have skills,

but working as a team is even more important," Kakashi explained. "When you act on your own, you put the rest of your team in danger."

Kakashi let go of Sasuke and stood up. He walked over to the boulder. For the first time, Naruto saw there were names carved into the stone.

"Look at this marker," the jonin said sadly. "These are the heroes of our village."

"That's gonna be me someday!" Naruto cried. "I want to be a hero too!"

"Naruto, you don't understand," Kakashi said. "These heroes all died in battle. One was my best friend. This stone is a memorial to them."

Everyone was silent. Naruto had thought

Kakashi was just weird, but now he understood him a little better. The test was tough because being a ninja was tough. It wasn't all just about excitement and adventure. This was serious training that could save their lives someday in battle.

Kakashi turned to them. "All right, I'm giving you one last chance. This next test will be harder than a little game with bells."

Naruto felt like cheering. Another chance!

The jonin nodded toward the lunch boxes. "I'll be fair. Sakura and Sasuke, you can eat. But no sharing food with Naruto. He goes hungry."

"Why?" Sakura asked.

"It's his own fault," Kakashi explained.

"He tried to keep the lunch all for himself. If either of you feeds him, you fail. Do you understand?"

"Yes, Sensei," Sakura said. Then Kakashi vanished into the trees.

7

SAKURA AND SASUKE quietly picked up their lunch boxes and began to eat. Naruto tried not to let it bug him. He was happy to get another chance, and he didn't want to mess up.

But his stomach was another story. It growled loudly.

"No big deal," Naruto said. "I can go without lunch, no problem."

Sasuke looked up at him. Then he held up his lunch box.

"Here," he said simply.

Sakura freaked out. "You can't give Naruto

your lunch! Master Kakashi will fail you!"

"I'm not worried," Sasuke said. "He's probably miles away by now. We all need our strength if we're going to work together to get those bells."

He nodded at Naruto. "Better eat. You're no good to us if you're weak."

Sakura couldn't believe it. Sasuke was breaking the rules! She didn't want to get in trouble, but Sasuke made a good point. Naruto needed his strength. And if Sasuke got caught, Sakura wouldn't pass the test anyway. Kakashi was right. All three of them needed to work together to pass.

Without a word, she handed her lunch box to Naruto.

"Thanks!" Naruto said.

Suddenly, a loud **WOOSH!** echoed through the field. Kakashi appeared.

"Oh no!" Sakura wailed.

Naruto groaned.

Sasuke clenched his fists. He had been fooled again.

Kakashi grinned. **"YOU PASS!"** he shouted.

Sakura's face was frozen in shock. Naruto's face was screwed up in a confused grimace. Sasuke gave his sensei a dark look. It was probably another of Kakashi's tricks.

Sakura spoke first. "We pass? But why?"

"Because you three took a giant step forward," Kakashi told them. "Up until now, you did everything I said without question. A true ninja looks for the hidden meanings within hidden meanings. Those who break the rules are lower than **GARBAGE.** But those who don't support the members of their team are even lower than that. You

three finally learned that, so you shared your lunch with Naruto."

"Wow," Naruto said. "That's kind of cool."

"This test is now over," Kakashi said. "You all pass! Squad Seven's first mission starts tomorrow."

"Woo-hoo!" Naruto cheered. "I did it! I'm a ninja! I'm a ninja! Yeah! All right!"

When Naruto stopped cheering, he saw

Sakura and Sasuke walking away.

"Uh, guys? I'm still tied up here," Naruto called out. "Guys?! COME BACK!"

73

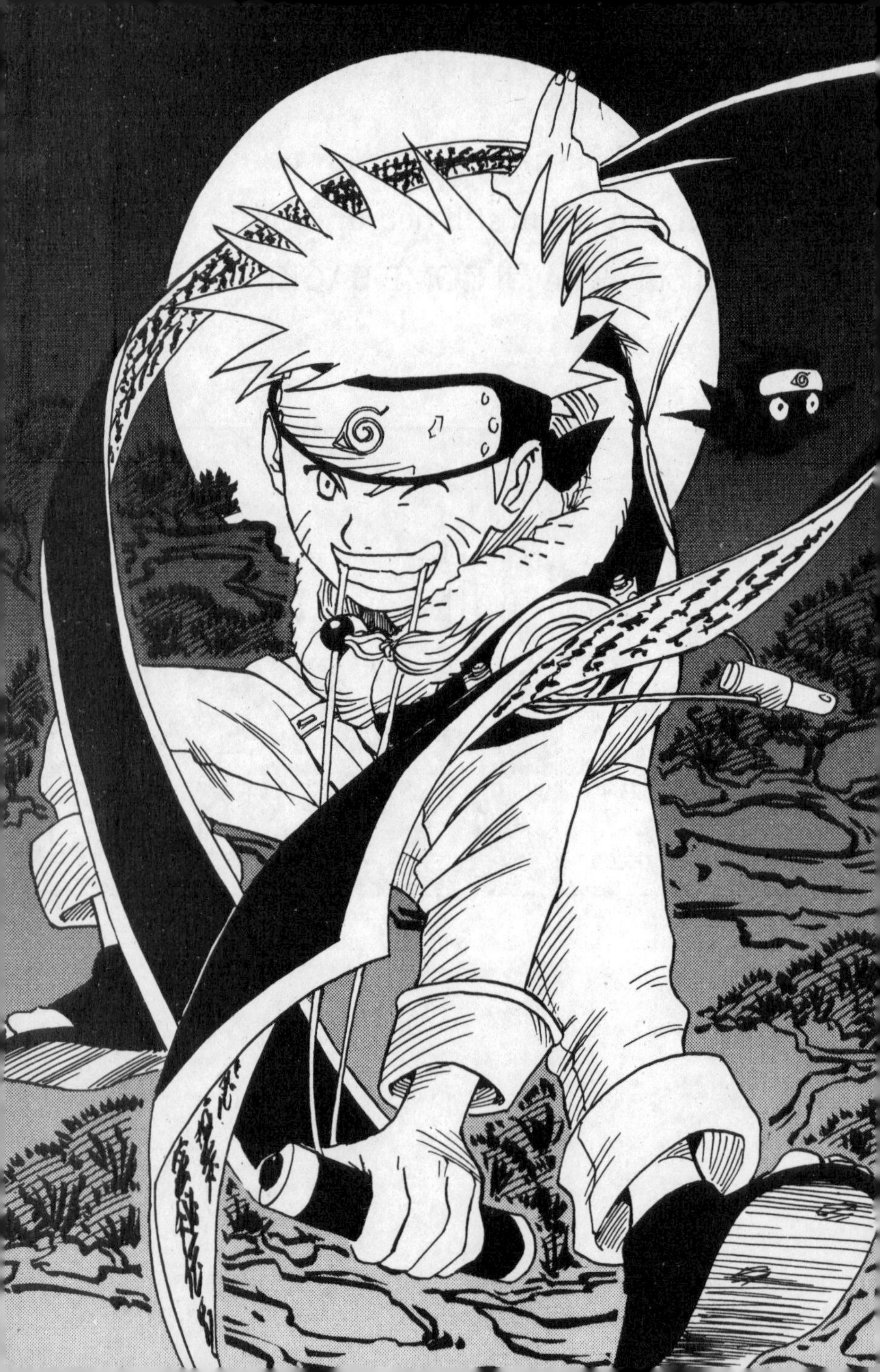

Ninja Terms

Hokage

The leader and protector of the Village Hidden in the Leaves. Only the strongest and wisest ninja can achieve this rank.

Jutsu

Jutsu means "arts" or "techniques." Sometimes referred to as *ninjutsu*, which means more specifically the jutsu of a ninja.

Bunshin

Translated as "doppelganger," this is the art of creating multiple versions of yourself.

Sensei

Teacher

Shuriken

A ninja weapon, a throwing star

About the Authors

Author/artist **Masashi Kishimoto** was born in 1974 in rural Okayama Prefecture, Japan. After spending time in art college, he won the Hop Step Award for new manga artists with his manga *Karakuri* (Mechanism). Kishimoto decided to base his next story on traditional Japanese culture. His first version of *Naruto*, drawn in 1997, was a one-shot story about fox spirits; his final version, which debuted in *Weekly Shonen Jump* in 1999, quickly became the most popular ninja manga in Japan. This book is based on that manga.

· · · · · ·

Tracey West is the author of more than 150 books for children and young adults, including the *Pixie Tricks* and *Scream Shop* series. An avid fan of cartoons, comic books, and manga, she has appeared on the New York Times Best Seller List as the author of the Pokémon chapter book adaptations. She currently lives with her family in New York State's Hudson Valley.

The Story of Naruto continues in:
Chapter Book 3
The Worst Job

Naruto and his friends from the Ninja Academy
get their first mission. They have to protect a
man named Mr. Tazuna, a famous bridge builder,
while they escort him to the village where he'll
be working on his next project. That means
Naruto gets to leave the Village Hidden in the
Leaves for the first time in his life. But the world
outside Konoha is a big and scary place!

COLLECT THEM ALL!

#1 THE BOY NINJA

#2 THE TESTS OF A NINJA

COMING SOON!

#3 THE WORST JOB

#4 THE SECRET PLAN

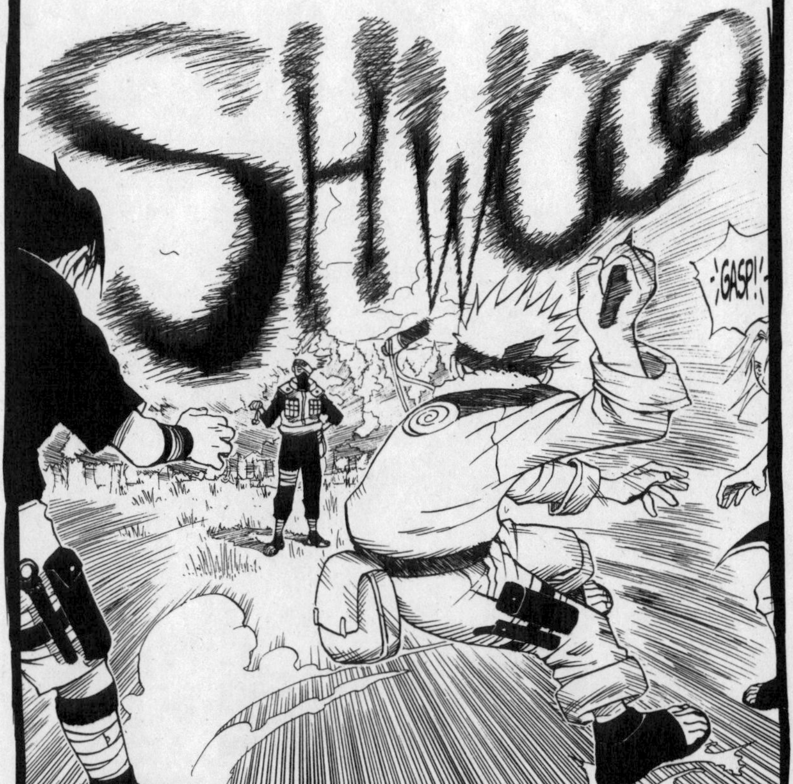
SHWOOO
GASP!